HARBINGERS 5

The Revealing

Bill Myers

Frank Peretti, Angela Hunt, and Alton Gansky

BILL MYERS

Published by Amaris Media International.
Copyright © 2015 Bill Myers
Cover Design: Angela Hunt
Photo © alextype

ISBN: 978-0692448328
ISBN: 0692448322

For more information, visit us on the Web:
www.harbingersseries.com

HARBINGERS

A novella series by
Bill Myers, Frank Peretti, Angela Hunt, and Alton Gansky

In this fast-paced world with all its demands, the four of us wanted to try something new. Instead of the longer novel format, we wanted to write something equally as engaging but that could be read in one or two sittings—on the plane, waiting to pick up the kids from soccer, or as an evening's read.

We also wanted to play. As friends and seasoned novelists, we thought it would be fun to create a game we could participate in together. The rules were simple:

Rule #1

Each of us would write as if we were one of the characters in the series:

Bill Myers would write as Brenda, the street-hustling tattoo artist who sees images of the future.

Frank Peretti would write as the professor, the atheist ex-priest ruled by logic.

Angela Hunt would write as Andi, the professor's brilliant-but-geeky assistant who sees inexplicable patterns.

Alton Gansky would write as Tank, the naïve, big-hearted jock with a surprising connection to a healing power.

Rule #2

Instead of the four of us writing one novella together (we're friends but not crazy), we would write it like a TV series. There would be an overarching story line into which we'd plug our individual novellas, with each story written from our character's point of view.

Bill's first novella, *The Call*, set the stage. It was followed by Frank's, *The Haunted*, Angela's *The Sentinels*, and Alton's *The Girl*. And now we return to Bill for the next cycle with *The Revealing*, as pieces begin tying together and amping up.

There you have it. We hope you'll find these as entertaining in the reading as we did in the writing.

Bill, Frank, Angie, and Al

Chapter 1

"What're you sketchin' now?" Cowboy asked.

I flipped my notebook shut like some kid caught with porn.

The big guy smirked. "You know, Miss Brenda, you don't have to keep hidin' your gift under a bushel."

I gave him a look. He gave me one of his good ol' boy shrugs. Daniel, who's sittin' on my other side, stifles a giggle.

I shoot him a look. "You think that's funny?"

He grins and imitates Cowboy's shrug.

I scowl. But the truth is I like that grin. It don't happen much, but whenever it does, it warms somethin' up inside me.

The sketch is a blue, velvet armchair. It's got peeling gold paint on its arms. I've been seeing it ever since we got on the plane to Rome. Never left my head. Not during the twelve hour flight with its crap food and rerun movies, not during Mr. Toad's wild taxi ride from Di Vinci airport to the Vatican, and not as we sat on this butt-numbing wood bench listening to the professor lay into some pimply-faced, man-boy receptionist.

"Well, look again." The old man waved at the computer screen. "Cardinal Hartmann. You do know what a Cardinal is, do you not? *Cardinal* Hartmann invited us to this location at this particular date and this particular time to—"

"*Mi scusi*, Signor, but you cannot have an appointment with—"

"Blast it all, don't tell me what I can and cannot have."

"But, such a thing, it is not—"

"I'm sorry, are you part of some special needs program?"

"Professor . . ." As usual, Andi, his ever-cheerful assistant, stepped in to try and prove her boss was a human being. As usual, the odds were not in her favor.

Meanwhile, Daniel scooted off the bench to get another drink of water. At least that's what I figured. But the way he cocked his head upwards like he was listening, told me one of his 'friends' was around.

Miss Congeniality continued smoothing things over. "What the professor means is, we've just come from the airport. In fact we haven't even gone to our hotel because Cardinal Hartmann sent a very urgent and very personal request for us to visit him today."

All true. It hadn't even been a month since the professor sent the Cardinal that scroll with the fancy writing on it. The one some kid, supposedly from another universe, gave us. I know, I know, long story and I'm not in the mood. The point is, this Cardinal guy, who used to be the professor's mentor back when the professor believed in God, begged us to come. He sweetened the deal by e-mailing each of us plane tickets. And since I couldn't cash them in, and since neither me nor Daniel have ever been out of the country, and since the professor pulled some strings to get us some fast passports . . . well, here we were with our ol' pals—stuck in some back-room reception area that smelled like old men and floor wax.

I glanced over to Daniel. He'd passed the water fountain and stood at a wooden door built into the wall. Hardly visible. He looked back at me like he wanted something.

What? I mouthed.

He just stood there.

"*What?*"

Meanwhile, the professor cranked up his personality to Super-Jerk. "Okay, you do that."

The receptionist had gotten up and was heading out of the room.

"Only make sure you bring back someone with rudimentary communication skills."

Daniel cleared his throat, real loud to get everyone's attention. We turned to him as he reached for the door. He pushed it open and motioned for us to join him.

"What is it now?" the professor said. "Do you wish for us to follow? Do you believe there is something inside there?"

Daniel sighed like it was obvious. And for him it probably was. Cause, like it or not, the kid heard things we never heard. Saw things we never saw. And whether the professor believed in any type of "higher power" or not made no difference. Our last couple road trips made it clear Daniel was connected to something.

So, without another word, Dr. Stuffy-Butt headed over to join the boy. Something was up and he knew it.

So did Cowboy. "What's goin' on little fella?" the big jock asked as he rose to his feet.

Daniel pointed to the open doorway. It was dark but you could just make out some narrow steps. Me and Andi glanced at each other then got up and followed. None of us knew what was going on in that little head of his, but whatever it was, it wouldn't hurt to pay attention.

Chapter 2

"Surely you're not serious?"

"Have I ever lied to you before?"

"Other than matters pertaining to God?"

Cardinal Hartmann waved the professor off with a boney, arthritic hand. "Please, James, do spare us your sophomoric wit. If I'd taught you anything, was it not to put aside your prejudices? Weigh all the facts and only then reach a reasonable conclusion."

The professor wasn't thrilled about being lectured in front of us but I didn't mind. It was good to see someone other than me putting him in his place.

We'd found the frail, old priest stashed away in some musty little apartment on the third floor. If it wasn't for Daniel's inside info we'd never have gotten to him . . . or dodged the locals who would have busted us for skulking around. Even then, it took twenty, maybe thirty minutes to wind through all the halls and stairs before we found him.

The assistant who'd opened the door for us was even skinnier than Hartmann. He wore thick, Coke-bottle glasses that hadn't been cleaned in years. He didn't say anything, just greeted us with a polite nod and ushered us inside.

Hartmann sat in the center of the room. He was hunched over in the exact chair I'd been sketching all these hours. He was too old to stand and greet us. And when the professor tried to shake his hand, he refused, laughing it off about being a closet germophobe. There was something more, but I couldn't put my finger on it.

Over on the desk was the scroll the professor had sent the Cardinal. But so far no one had brought it up. Instead, we were sitting in some broken down apartment listening to some broken down priest telling us an unbelievable story. Most of it had to do with the small display case the assistant had wheeled in. And the rusty spearhead inside.

The professor tried to be cool, but you could tell he wasn't happy. "Can you honestly tell me with a straight face that the artifact before us is the reason Hitler started World War II?"

"No." Hartmann shook his head. "Though my brothers here insist upon this one's authenticity, there was another lance with greater credentials in Habsburg Treasure House Museum in Vienna. That was the one Hitler insisted upon owning—the one both he and Himmler believed had great, supernatural powers. A fact underlined by Hitler's immediate visit to the museum to take possession of it when his troops marched into Vienna."

The professor said nothing—a first, as far as I could tell. He just sat there, eyeing his old mentor, wondering if the priest had lost his mind. And the more he talked, the more I figured he might be right.

"Because of Hitler's deep involvement with the occult, he believed who ever controlled the Spear of Destiny would control the world."

Andi motioned to the display case. "The Spear of Destiny. The one that supposedly pierced Christ's side at his crucifixion?"

"That is correct. Because it was used to kill God's Son and because some of His blood remained on it, Hitler believed whoever owned the spear would be invincible."

We sat in silence a long moment until the professor answered. "Poppycock."

"Perhaps. But do keep in mind that it is the exact spear the Emperor Constantine claimed gave him his power. Then there is the overwhelming evidence that Charlemagne actually slept with it. Finally, we have the minor fact that over forty-five emperors for over a thousand years possessed it and claimed it facilitated their ability to rule.

"Proving absolutely nothing."

"And the very day the Nazis lost the spear to General Patton, who later returned it to Vienna, was the very day Hitler committed suicide."

"That may be true," Andi said. "But as you said that's not this spear here. That's the one in Vienna."

"Yes and no. Granted, it is not this spear. However I do not believe the spear Patton returned to Vienna is the same spear Hitler stole."

"But you just said—"

"The Nazis were notorious for creating replicas of the treasures they stole. Paintings, statues, religious artifacts—"

"And spears," Cowboy said.

"That is correct."

Cowboy stole a glance to Andi, no doubt hoping she noticed his powers of deduction.

She didn't.

"So if this isn't the real spear," she said, "and the one in Vienna isn't the real one, then—"

There was a knock on the door. Andi stopped as Hartmann raised his hand for us to be quiet. There was another knock. Again he motioned for us to be silent. After, what seemed forever, the footsteps faded down the hall.

When they were gone Hartmann answered Andi's question. "That is the very reason we have summoned your team here."

"Team?" I couldn't help but smirk. "I wouldn't go calling us a team."

The priest looked at me. I held his gaze but he didn't blink.

He answered. "We have decided you are the ones called to find and retrieve the real Spear of Destiny."

"We?" I said. "Who's *we*?"

He started to answer, then stopped and shook his head.

"And what's all this got to do with the scroll?" I nodded to the scroll sitting on the desk.

"Everything. And more."

"Yeah? Like what?"

"You shall find out soon enough."

I kept staring. There was something about him. He seemed honest enough, I'll give him that, but there was something.

The professor gave a heavy sigh. "So you brought us half way around the world to find some mythical artifact with a questionable history that may or may not even exist."

"Oh, it exists, James."

The professor continued. "And to what purpose are we retrieving it? To add yet another item to your obscenely bloated Vatican collection?"

"No. To prevent the others from adding it to theirs."

"Others?" Andi said.

The priest nodded. "Hitler is dead, this is true."

"At last, a verified fact," the professor said.

"But there is another force far more powerful." He turned to the professor. "The very one your overinflated sense of logic keeps denying. One whose power grows stronger every day."

"I kinda got lost," Cowboy said. "What force are we talkin' about?"

"You've already encountered it. More than once." He turned to Andi. "On your beaches."

Andi frowned. "All those dying fish and birds?"

"And earlier. As far back as your first meeting at the Institute."

"The Psychic Institute?" I asked.

"It was one of their training grounds."

"Sridhar," I said. "The kid mentioned something about an organization. What did he call it?"

A moment then Cowboy beamed. "The Gate."

"That's right," Andi said. "The Gate."

Cowboy beamed brighter. She didn't notice.

The priest continued: "Should the spear fall into their hands they shall—"

"—rule the world and make us all their slaves." The professor's voice dripped with sarcasm. "No doubt ushering in the post-apocalyptic nightmare that will destroy all mankind."

Hartmann looked at him then answered. "No, not yet. They still need to secure the appropriate items and people. But possessing the spear will greatly expedite their plans."

Daniel gave a start and spun to the door.

"What's the matter little guy?" Cowboy said.

The priest lowered his voice and spoke quickly. "We haven't much time. It is imperative you find the spear and bring it here as quickly as possible."

"But . . ." Andi frowned. "How? Where do we start? Where do we—"

There was another knock on the door. Hartmann traded looks with his assistant who nodded and shuffled over to answer it.

Hartmann turned back to Andi and whispered. "The Appian Way. The Catacombs."

"The Catacombs," the professor scoffed. "Aren't we being just a bit melo—"

More knocking, louder.

The assistant reached for the handle but was a fraction too late. The door flew open and five wannabe linebackers stormed in. We jumped to our feet ready to defend ourselves.

"No," Hartmann cried. "Do not resist them. Our meeting is over."

The first fellow grabbed me. I swore and tried to land a good kick, but he saw it coming. The second guy reached for Andi. Big mistake. Cowboy saw it and threw all 275 pounds at him. They crashed to the floor and traded punches.

"Don't resist," the priest kept shouting. "We have finished. Do not resist."

I searched for Daniel who was off to the side, safe.

"Unhand me, you Neanderthal!" the professor was yelling at the third man.

The other two had joined the one fighting Cowboy. Even at that the odds weren't exactly in their favor.

"Don't resist! Bjorn Christensen, there is no need to resist."

The sound of his name brought Cowboy up short. He turned to the priest.

"We have concluded our business. There is no need to resist."

They got Cowboy to his feet. "Okay, fellas," he said. "Take it easy. I heard the man, take it easy."

They guided us to the open door. I looked over my shoulder to see Daniel trailing close behind. We'd barely made it into the hallway, before Hartmann called after us. "The feast is in the kitchen."

I turned to him.

He nodded and repeated, "The feast is in the kitchen."

His assistant also nodded, then smiled, then shut the door . . . as the big boys escorted us down the hall.

Chapter 3

I wanted Daniel to see some of Rome, especially the Coliseum. We caught a glimpse of it as our taxi shot past. I even got a couple of blurred selfies. But it wasn't quite the same. Still, it would be somethin' to show Social Services next time they come snoopin' around seein' if I'm a fit guardian.

It took us half an hour to get from the Vatican to the creepy church basement full of human skeletons. Which, to be honest, was probably more exciting to a ten-year-old kid than a bunch of old ruins. And we're not talkin' one or two skeletons. According to Andi, our self-appointed tour guide, and with a little help from Wikipedia on her cell phone:

"The crypt consists of 3754 bodies, all Capuchin Monks who fled the French Revolution and took refuge in the church immediately above us. The Capuchin order separated from the Franciscan monks in 1525 in the belief that they needed to be more austere. Oh, and here's something you'll find incredibly fascinating . . ."

"I'm sure we will," the professor muttered.

"Cappuccino coffee actually received its name from the color of the monks' robes."

On and on she went. And just when it couldn't get any more boring, she went on some more. 'Course Cowboy hung on her every word, but me and Daniel couldn't care less. Who cares about the history of a bunch of dead monks when their actual skeletons were all around? And not whole skeletons. They were separated into lots of feet, legs, ribs, and skulls. Piles and piles of skulls.

Some were used to build altars. Others made up a giant clock with toes and fingers. There were chandeliers made from hundreds of vertebrae and hipbones. Nearly every wall was covered with complex patterns of bones.

And not just one room. I counted six. Each one labeled. Things like: *The Crypt of Skulls. The Crypt of Pelvises. The Crypt of Leg Bones.*

Yeah, it creeped me out a little. But Daniel's wide-eyed wonder said he was in kid heaven.

"Anybody see anything?" the professor asked. "Clues? Diagrams? Something to tell me this isn't a complete waste of my time?"

Nobody saw nothing.

Except Andi. "Guys, check this out." She was

looking at a wall up ahead. It was covered with arm bones that made up different squares and boxes."

"Lovely," the professor said.

"No, don't you see it?" Andi asked.

He didn't. No one did.

Except Cowboy. "It's a window box," he said. "Like my mom use to have to show off her knick-knacks."

"Well, that's one possibility," Andi said. "Or . . . ?"

She waited but there were no takers.

"It's a floor plan. Don't you see it? There's the front door down here at the bottom. It's even open. Here's the entry hall with one set of stairs. The living room, hallway with another set of stairs, dining room, kitchen. And over here is . . ." she slowed to a stop.

"Over here is what?" Cowboy asked.

She got real quiet. "I've seen this before."

"Where?" Cowboy said.

We waited. Daniel reached up and took my hand.

When Andi continued her voice was a little unsteady. "When we were up in Washington State . . . It's the house. The one that kept haunting Van Epps, the professor's friend. It's the floor plan to the house."

Chapter 4

I grabbed shots of the floor plan with my cell phone .
. . which pissed off some caretaker . . . which I
ignored . . . which got him in my face . . . which got
my elbow in his gut . . . which got us thrown out . . .

Which was getting to be a habit.

I squinted as we stepped out into the late
afternoon sun. "Now what?"

"Cardinal Hartmann said catacombs," Andi said.
"Not catacomb, singular, but catacombs, plural."

"There's more?"

"Actually, 186 miles of them."

"One hundred eighty-six miles of—"

"I suggest we continue next by exploring the Domitilla Catacombs," she said. "They're quite close and one of the oldest and best cared for."

"How many rooms?" I asked.

"Tunnels," she said.

"How many tunnels?"

"Nine miles."

I swore. The professor joined me. But it didn't stop our personal cheerleader from leading us forward.

When we got to the entrance, the ticket guy at the door shook his head. "*Chiuso,*" he said. "Too late. Come back tomorrow."

Andi pleaded, said we were on an urgent mission. The professor even played his priest card (which had expired a few decades earlier). Nothing worked. The guard shook his head, pretending he didn't understand . . . till I slipped a handful of Euros into his palm. He understood that perfectly.

Andi had reconnected to Wikipedia. So as we headed down the narrow steps into the cooler air, she resumed the tour. "There are roughly forty catacombs built under the city. Despite legends that Christians hid in them during the time of persecution, it is more probable that due to restricted land use, as well as their insistence upon being buried instead of cremated, these underground chambers were dug to serve primarily as cemeteries."

"More dead bodies," the professor sighed.

"Actually, in these particular catacombs there are indeed a few remaining. However, in the others, the bones have long since been removed."

"No doubt sold as picture frames," he said.

Daniel giggled.

"Named after St. Domitilla, their history is as lengthy as their tunnels and tributaries which, by the way, are stacked on top of one another up to four levels high. Now, coming up to our right you'll note a delightful fresco painted by . . . by . . ." She lost reception. She waved her phone around to find the signal. The professor gave another sigh—this time out of gratitude.

"Hey, check out these symbols," Cowboy said. I crossed over to look at his wall. "Here's a guy with a lamb on his shoulders. I bet that's Jesus. And here, look, it's a dove with some sort of branch."

"That would be an olive branch," Andi said. "Together the dove and olive branch would represent divine peace with God. In fact, in Greek, the very word *cemetery* means 'place of rest,' and in the Hebrew—"

"They're here," Daniel said.

It was the first words he'd spoken all afternoon.

"Who?" I said.

He pointed down the tunnel behind us.

"Someone's coming? Who?" I asked.

"For us."

The bare bulbs hanging along the ceiling gave off plenty of light, but I didn't see anything

"Listen," the professor said.

I strained to hear. There were footsteps. Running. And getting closer. And hushed voices speaking a language I couldn't make out.

I traded looks with the others.

Daniel didn't wait for a discussion. He grabbed my hand and yanked me forward. We started down the tunnel. The others followed.

"Faster," he whispered. "Faster."

We broke into a run for, I don't know, forty, fifty yards, when he darted to the right. It was a little niche off to the side. Unlit, almost invisible. Stairs were cut into the wall. Steep and narrow. Almost a ladder. He started up them. I hesitated, then followed. Then the others, and finally the professor.

As we climbed, pieces of rocks crumbled and fell.

"Be careful up there," he hissed.

The steps got steeper. The sides of the wall came so close they touched you. After a few minutes or so I saw some blue-green light above us. Parking lot lights. The sun had already set and the parking lot lights had come on.

Down below a man's voice shouted, "Up there!" It sounded Swedish or something. "You there. Halt!"

We kept going, not bothering to answer.

The light above got brighter. Pretty soon you could see it was coming through a round opening. In another minute we arrived at an iron grate.

The good news was there was a way out. The bad news was the grate wouldn't budge.

"Keep going," the professor whispered. "Why have we stopped?"

The voices below got closer.

Me and Daniel both tried pushing against the grate with all we had. "It's no good," I said. "They got it locked."

Cowboy tried squeezing past. "Maybe, if I could just—" But things were too cramped. No way could he get past us.

"Doesn't matter," I said. "It won't budge." I gave it one last push. "It's welded shut or something."

"We're trapped?" Andi asked.

I swore and nodded . . . until I spotted the girl.

Her face so close to mine I gasped. It was the kid from that other world, Cowboy's and Daniel's friend. She was on her hands and knees, hunched inside a small tunnel connected to ours. A tunnel I was sure hadn't been there till now.

Cowboy saw her, too. "Helsa?" He moved up closer. "Littlefoot, is that you?"

She smiled. Even in the dim light I could see the silver in her eyes sparkle. A sure sign she was happy.

"What's going on up there?" the professor whispered.

"We missed you," Cowboy said. You could hear the softness in his voice. "You come back to visit?"

She nodded then reached out for Daniel's hand. He let her take it and she pulled him into the tunnel. Once inside, he turned to help me. I took his hand and he pulled me in. I did the same for Cowboy, who did the same for Andi, who did the same for the professor.

Now we were all in the side tunnel crawling as fast as we could. No talking. No sound. Just lots of hands and knees scraping along the rocks. I felt something long and smooth in the wall beside me. Then it got bumpy, then ridges. Ribs. I yanked back my hand, not wanting to feel more.

Finally, the girl came to a stop.

The professor whispered, "What's going—"

"Shh," Daniel said.

For once in his life the professor obeyed. A good thing, too, because the men behind us had reached the top.

One of them was speaking Swedish again.

Another answered.

We held our breaths.

You could hear them strain and push against the grate as they kept talking and getting madder.

Finally the first one shouted in his heavy accent, "Hello? Is anyone there? Is there anyone who can hear us?"

We kept silent.

They talked some more. They pushed and grunted some more. Finally they gave up and started back down.

The girl motioned for us to wait till the sound of their climbing had nearly faded. Then she started forward again and we followed. After another minute or so the tunnel angled up. A moment later we were out in the open surrounded by bushes and shrubs.

It was good to finally stand up and breathe. And despite my promise never to light up around Daniel, I pulled a cigarette from my pocket. Things were eerily quiet. We were pretty far from the parking lot, but could still see each other's faces in the shadows. Except for the girl's.

She was gone.

Chapter 5

"Hello?"

"Signora, the taxi, it is here."

"We'll be there in a sec," I said.

"For your bags, shall I send him up?"

"No, we're good." I hung up the phone and faced the others. They'd been in Daniel's and my room the last forty-five minutes begging us to stay.

"But you just can't leave," Cowboy whined.

"Watch us." I crossed to the bathroom and dumped the free soap and shampoo into my bag.

"But what about the spear and the diagram and the cardinal?"

"And saving the world?" Andi added.

The professor answered, "She's more concerned in

saving her inconsequential derrière."

"You're one to talk," I said as I reentered the room. "I'm surprised you even bothered to come."

"Call it scientific curiosity."

"And the scroll," Cowboy said. "Remember he was going to tell us what it meant."

"Which he didn't." I opened the mini-fridge, grabbed the two Cokes but left the booze—too many bad memories.

"We really need you, Miss Brenda."

I slammed the fridge. "I got Daniel to look out for now."

"And some enormous guilt to work off."

I turned back to the professor. "Meaning?"

"We all saw what you went through at the Institute. All those fears . . . all that guilt."

"Professor," Andi warned.

"Not that I fault you. It must be a tremendous burden—giving up your spawn, knowing you were an unfit mother to raise it."

The muscles in my jaw tightened.

He motioned to Daniel. "It doesn't take a genius to see the boy is simply serving as a surrogate, a vain attempt on your part to work off all that—"

I didn't hear much after that—saw nothing but his smug face as I sprang at it. I landed a couple good blows before Cowboy pulled me off. "Hey, hey, Miss Brenda! Miss Brenda, come on now!"

When things settled down, I turned to my backpack and finished shoving clothes into it. Daniel was already at the door, sitting peacefully on his own pack.

"She's not going anywhere," the professor muttered. He was nursing what would likely be a shiner. "The tickets are non-refundable. She can't leave until the date of departure, just like the rest of us."

"Is that true?" Cowboy asked.

"Not without buying another ticket," Andi said.

"Which means cash," the professor said. "Something of which I'm sure she's a bit lacking."

I reached into my pocket and tossed his American Express back to him.

Now he leaped at me.

"Professor!" Andi and Cowboy shouted. It took both of them to stop him.

I zipped up my backpack and headed for the door. "Let's go, Daniel." But before I reached it, there was a knock. I glanced to the others, then opened it.

Two men in silver sunglasses stood there. "Taxi?" the biggest said. There was no missing his Swedish accent. I tried slamming the door but his size-14s blocked it. I yelled and swore as they threw it open and stormed in.

Cowboy was on his feet, doing what he did best. He flew across the room, decking the first guy, knocking off his glasses. We all stood and stared. And for good reason. The big Swede lay on the floor with no eyes. That's right, his sockets were completely empty.

The second guy took advantage of our shock and landed a good punch into Cowboy's gut and then his face. Not enough to ruin him, but enough to make his point.

"Run!" Cowboy shouted to us. "All of you, run!"

I didn't need a second invitation. I grabbed Daniel and we headed for the stairs, the professor right behind. Andi needed more convincing. "Tank!"

"Go Andi! Go!"

We got to the bottom of the steps, raced through the lobby and out onto the street. Wheels screeched and I spun around just in time to see a taxi mini-van. It barely missed us. The driver shouted through the passenger window, "Taxi?" He had a black beard and a Middle Eastern accent so thick I could barely understand.

"What?" I said.

"Taxi? Taxi?"

I saw Cowboy stagger from the lobby, a little worse for wear.

"Taxi?"

"No." I turned from Cowboy back to the driver. "I mean, yes. Maybe. You'll go to the airport?"

"Defeats," he said.

"What?"

"I take you to defeats."

"Defeats? What are you—"

"No. Defeats! Defeats!"

"The feets?" Cowboy asked. "You want to take us to the feets?"

"Yes, yes. Get in. All of you. Hurry."

"Whose feet?" Andi said.

"Are you speaking of more skeletons?" the professor asked. "The Catacombs?"

"No! No! Defeats!"

The hotel doors flew open and the two Swedes stormed out. During the brawl the second one had also lost his glasses. His eye sockets were as empty as his partner's. And yet they raced toward us like they could see perfectly.

"Some folks." Cowboy sighed. "I try to be polite but they just won't take a hint." He positioned himself at the back of the taxi between us and them for another round.

"Hurry!" the driver shouted. "All of you, get in!"

The men kept coming. "Stay calm," the first said. "No one need be hurt."

"Get in!" the driver kept yelling. "Everyone, get in!"

I threw open the back door and shoved Daniel inside. Andi raced to the other door as the professor squeezed in beside me and Daniel crawled into the rear seat.

"Stay calm. No one need be—"

"Cowboy!" I shouted.

The first guy came at him. But the second headed around front for the driver, who panicked and dropped the van into reverse. A good idea, except for the first guy. The taxi slammed into him and knocked him to the ground. The wheels bumped over something that was not a curb. And when I looked out the back window, there was no bad guy.

Cowboy dropped to his knees, looking under the car. "Mister? Mister, are you okay?"

Off in the distance, I heard a police siren. "Cowboy," I shouted. "Get in!"

"But, he's—"

Meanwhile, Bad Guy #2 had reached the driver's window and was banging on it. "Stay calm. No one need be hurt. Stay calm. No one need be hurt."

"Now!" I shouted at Cowboy. "Get in, now!"

Reluctantly, he rose, headed to the front door and climbed in.

"Stay calm. No one need be hurt. Stay calm. No one—"

The driver stomped on the gas, throwing the

attacker to the side while again bouncing the rear wheel over his partner.

"I take you to defeats," The driver shouted as he picked up speed. "Defeats in the kitchen!"

"What are you saying?" the professor demanded. "What defeats?"

"No," Andi said. "Not defeats." She turned to the driver. "Are you saying *the feast?*"

"Yes, yes! De feasts, it is in the kitchen! That is what I am saying!"

She looked to the professor. "'The feast is in the kitchen.' Cardinal Hartmann's parting words."

"Yes, yes! Defeats in the kitchen. Hurry! We must hurry!"

I looked out the back window. The bad guys were nearly a block away. And the one we'd run over twice? He was getting back to his feet.

Chapter 6

For half an hour we'd been playing Q and A with the taxi driver. The problem was, he did most of the questioning.

"Why do you persist in asking us?" the professor called from the back seat. "You seem to be the one with all the answers."

"'The feet are in the kitchen.'" Cowboy chuckled. "That's a good one."

"I do not know, that is why I am asking. You said the airport but there is no airport on the beach."

"Beach?" I said. "Why are we going to the beach?"

The professor interrupted. "Cardinal Hartmann instructed you to pick us up, did he not?"

"I know no Hartmann. I know very little of

nothing."

"But you knew where we'd be," Andi said.

"I know only what I hear."

"From whom?" the professor asked.

"From my head. Words. I hear words. And sometimes, as you may tell, I do not always hear so well."

Cowboy chuckled, "The feet are in the kitchen."

There was a loud thud on the roof and we gave a start. I looked out the windows. Nothing to see but the thick blanket of fog we'd been driving through for the past few minutes.

"We're at a beach?" I said.

"Yes, yes. But as I have told you, there is no airport at the beach."

"Then why are you—"

There was another thump, and then another. I saw something bounce off the hood.

"What was that?" the professor demanded.

More thumping.

"What is going on?"

"That is what I keep asking you."

I looked out the side window. There were dozens of birds, mostly seagulls, flapping around on the road.

"Well, will you look at that," Cowboy said.

One hit the windshield. Blood and feathers everywhere.

Andi shuddered. "That's gross."

The driver turned on his wipers. It pushed off most of the feathers but left a smear of blood that took several more swipes to get rid of. Another one hit the roof. And then another. They came faster, like a hail storm—hitting the roof, hood, windshield, the rear window.

The professor turned to look out back. "Remarkable," was all he said.

Another hit the windshield. So hard it left a spider web crack. Another one followed. Faster and faster. With the smearing blood and feathers the wipers couldn't keep up. Unable to see, the driver hit the brakes and we slid.

"Careful man!" the professor shouted.

But the birds were slippery. We veered into the other lane. No problem except for the one and only vehicle we'd seen on the road—a produce truck. It appeared out of nowhere through the fog. The driver blasted his horn. When I looked out the side window I was looking straight at him, straight into his terrified face.

It was close. We missed each other by only inches. Our car shot up and over a small embankment. We landed hard on the sand, bouncing several times before coming to a stop.

We sat a moment, catching our breath.

The birds continued to fall. Nonstop pounding.

"Everybody is okay?" the driver shouted over the noise.

We were—if "okay" meant being in the middle of a storm of falling birds. Everywhere we looked, they were falling and flapping.

"My grandparents' beach," Andi said. "It's like what happened on their beach."

The driver dropped the car in reverse and hit the gas. The wheels spun. The windshield cracked into another spider web. More blood and feathers.

"We can't stay in here!" the professor shouted.

"Where do we—"

"There!" the driver pointed to a bus stop or taxi

stand or something. Whatever it was, it had a roof and it was close.

The back window shattered. I grabbed Daniel and yanked him toward me, away from the raining glass.

"Hurry!" the driver shouted. "Go!"

We didn't need a second invitation. As soon as the professor threw open his door, I pushed him out and spun around for Daniel. "Come on!" I did my best to protect him as the two of us ran for cover. I got hit two, maybe three times, but nothing bad. Daniel, too, but he looked fine. Actually more than fine. Not that he was enjoying himself. But almost.

We got under the corrugated roof, which made the falling birds even louder. Cowboy followed with Andi tucked under one arm, the professor under the other. The driver stayed behind. Revving his engine, spinning his wheels.

Cowboy shouted to him over the noise. "Best you get out of there!"

The driver ignored him. It looked like he was going to go down with the ship.

Or not.

Suddenly, the wheels found traction and the taxi took off.

Cowboy cheered. Andi clapped. Of course they'd be happier if the driver had circled around to join us. But he didn't.

"Hey!" Cowboy shouted as the car bounced back onto the road. "Hey!"

"Return here at once!" the professor yelled. "You are not leaving us stranded!"

But the driver had other ideas. He swerved hard, sliding into a U-turn. He stomped on the gas, wheels spinning, until they caught and sent him racing back down the road toward the city.

The others shouted. I didn't bother.

In a minute or two the bird storm slowed to a stop. Now they just lay there, flapping and gasping for breath. I knelt down to take a better look.

Cowboy stooped to join me. "Wow."

I nodded.

"Look, they got no eyes."

I nodded. "Just like the fellows back at the hotel."

"And the birds and fish back at Andi's grandparents. Poor things."

I grabbed a twig and poked at one. It kept opening and closing its beak like it was trying to talk but no sounds came.

"Great," Andi sighed. I glanced up to see her peering out into the fog. "Now what do we do?"

Not a bad question. Considering the produce truck had been the only car we'd seen on the road. And houses? Forget it. At least none we could see in the fog.

Andi pulled out her phone and tried to get a signal. I stepped away from the group and lit a cigarette.

"What's that over there?" Cowboy said.

I followed his gaze up the beach. Through the grayness and off the right you could just make out some pillars of rock rising from the water. And to the left above the beach, a cliff thirty or forty feet high. But it wasn't the cliff that got my attention. It was the tiny squares of light coming from it.

"Are those . . . windows?" I squinted. "Is somebody living there?"

"Sure looks like it," Cowboy said. "Like them cliff homes the desert Indians built."

"Are you getting any reception?" the professor

asked Andi.

She shook her head. "Nothing."

"Looks like someone's got some real nice, beach-front property," Cowboy said.

The professor muttered something, then stepped out from under the covering. Without a word, he headed up the beach.

"Professor," Andi called, "where are you going?"

He shouted over his shoulder. "I have seen enough." He cursed as he tripped over a seagull and nearly fell. He motioned to the cliff. "If that's light coming from those windows it has electricity and most likely a telephone. And if it has a telephone I am calling a real taxi to take us to a real airport."

We traded looks. The feeling was unanimous. I butted out my cig, grabbed Daniel's hand and followed.

Chapter 7

A hundred yards up the beach and we were out of dead birds. The walk was short. But not short enough to stop Andi from chattering away with more fun-filled Spear of Destiny facts. Not that it wasn't interesting. But it had been a busy morning. A little quiet wouldn't hurt.

But, since quiet wasn't one of her high cards . . .

"There's one theory, quite popular, that says after Hitler made the duplicate of the spear, he shipped the original off, along with other priceless art treasures, to a special bunker in Antarctica."

"No kidding," Cowboy said.

"Yes. His idea was that should the Third Reich fail, the Spear would be there to empower the Fourth

Reich when it resurfaced."

"Wow," Cowboy said.

"And after the war, a secret German convoy returned the spear to a secret organization called The Knights of the Holy Lance whose sole purpose was to keep it hidden until the proper time."

"That's really impressive," Cowboy said.

Truth is, Andi could be reading the phone book and he'd be really impressed. Too bad. Cause the big guy was setting himself up for a massive heartbreak. And you didn't need someone like me to see that in his future.

By the time we got to the cliff, the cold dampness had worked its way through my thin, SoCal clothes. Not Daniel. He wore the UW sweatshirt Cowboy's uncle had given him. A little salt in Cowboy's wounds, since earlier he'd been bounced from the team for helping us.

"You okay?" I asked Daniel.

He nodded but I'm not sure he heard. He was too awed by the cliff and whatever was carved into it. Those little squares of light really had turned out to be windows. Two stories worth. Well, three if you count the dormer that stuck out above the center. It had the vague outline of one of those old Victorian houses. Strange. Stranger still, there was something familiar about it.

Once we got there the professor headed up the stone steps and knocked on a front door of thick, wooden planks.

There was no answer. We joined him as he knocked again.

Nothing.

He was about to try a third time when the door

suddenly opened. And there in front of us stood some old, jolly-faced nun. The moment she saw us she broke into a grin. The professor started to introduce himself, but it didn't matter. She opened the door wider and motioned us inside like we were old friends.

It was like stepping into a giant, elaborate cave. Even though it was carved into rock, the entry hall was like a real house. There was an antique bureau with mirror, a hall tree, a grandfather clock. To the right was a fancy staircase with polished wood. I couldn't put my finger on it, and maybe it was just my "gift," but I definitely felt I'd been there before.

"So," the professor was saying, "if you would be so kind as to allow us to make a phone call, we shall be out of your hair in no time."

The nun's smile grew bigger. She still didn't speak but motioned us toward some double doors. I glanced to Daniel. The kid was a pretty good barometer when it came to danger and he looked more intrigued than nervous.

We stepped through the doors and into what could only be a living room. Sofa, end tables, lamps. No feeling of being in a cave. Instead, it was all very Victorian . . . and very familiar.

"The house," Andi whispered.

We all looked to her.

"It's like the house in Washington."

The double doors behind us shut. I turned and the nun was gone. There was a quiet click of a lock. We traded looks.

Andi crossed back to the doors. "Hello?" She tapped on them. "Hello? If you could just tell us where the telephone is? Hello, are you there?"

The professor brushed past her and tried the handles. They didn't move. He shook them. "Come on." He pulled. He pushed. Then he stopped and took a step back. So did Andi. And for good reason.

The doors were . . . melting. And not just the doors. The wall around them. And the pictures on the wall and the shelves.

And the floor.

Starting at the doors, the floor was turning to liquid . . . which flowed toward us.

"Step away!" The professor motioned. "Everybody step away."

It seemed a pretty good idea and we all took several steps back.

It kept coming. Daniel gripped my hand. Not a good sign.

It flowed under a chair against the wall in front of us. The legs dissolved and the chair slumped into itself. Then it sank into the floor. Gone. Completely melted. The same with the nearby sofa.

"What's goin' on?" Cowboy said. "What's happening?"

If anyone had an answer, they weren't telling.

"To the other side of the room!" the professor ordered. "Quickly." We crossed the room and reached a single door at the opposite end. It was closed and locked. No problem. Cowboy leaned down and slammed into it with his shoulder. It budged, but not much. He tried again.

The tide of melting floor kept coming. By now half the place had dissolved—the sofa, end tables, lamps. But only for a second. Because a few yards behind all that melting, the room was getting solid again. Reshaping itself. It was the same room, but instead of rock, the far wall had changed into light-colored, oak paneling. Where the furniture had been, desks were appearing. Lots of them.

"Remarkable," the professor said.

"Everything's morphing," Andi said.

I turned to her. "It's what?"

"Everything is morphing into another reality."

Whatever she called it, it didn't help. The melting was closing in fast.

Cowboy finally broke down the door. He stared at the pieces, not happy with the damage he'd caused. The rest of us were just happy to get out of there.

We stepped into a short hallway—a dining room was just ahead with eight high-back chairs, dishes already set, and a fancy chandelier. Beyond that you could see a little kitchen with an eating area. To our right was a back set of steps.

"Which way?" Andi said.

After a quick look, the professor ordered, "The stairs."

We started up them. Everyone but Cowboy. He stayed at the broken door figuring how he could fix it.

"Tank!" Andi called.

He looked back to the living room. The melting tide had just about reached him. Figuring now was as good a time as any, he decided to join us.

Safe and out of the way, the professor stopped in the middle of the stairs to watch. We all did. The melting swept through the doorway, dissolving the broken door as it went. Not far behind the melting, the floor kept turning solid as more and more desks appeared. And what looked like, and I know this is crazy, but computer monitors with people beginning to appear in front of them.

The melting washed in and swirled around the base of the steps. They lurched, then dropped. They were also melting.

"Up here!" the professor shouted.

We scrambled up after him as the steps continued to slip and shift.

"Miss Brenda!"

I spun around. The step below Cowboy had given way. I threw out my hand to him. An idiot move. He could have dragged me down with him. But he hung on just long enough to steady himself before letting go and continuing.

We reached the top of the steps and another hallway.

The professor tried the first door. It opened easily. But . . . well, things were getting even weirder.

On the other side of the door, directly in front of us, was the outside of the same cliff house we'd just entered. We were back at beach level looking up at the same cliff house with the same stone steps leading to the same front door.

Behind us, the last of the stairway gave way and splashed into the liquid. The hallway was next.

"Come!" the professor shouted. He stepped outside onto the sand.

More crashing and splashing. The hallway was falling.

"Quickly!"

It seemed a pretty good idea.

Chapter 8

We stepped through the bedroom door and back onto the beach, leaving the melting hallway behind us.

It was a useless idea, but I figured I'd slow it down by reaching back and shutting the door. Only problem was there *was* no door. When I turned there was nothing but the beach and sea behind me.

"What the heck's goin' on?" Cowboy said. "Am I dreamin'?"

"If you are, we all are," I said.

Andi turned to the professor. "Do you suppose . . . is it possible we are experiencing some sort of multiverse?"

"A whatee verse?" Cowboy said. Then his face brightened. "Oh, like where you said Littlefoot is from. One of those higher dimensions all around us."

Andi shook her head. "Higher dimensions are

something entirely different.

"Like angels and stuff," I said.

The professor scoffed.

Andi ignored him. "Perhaps. Whereas the theory of the multiverse believes in an infinite number of realities, each branching off and forming another reality, whenever a decision is made."

"*Another reality.*" I motioned over my shoulder to the door, or where the door should be. "Is that what we saw in there? One reality changing to another?"

Andi frowned, then turned from the sea back to the cliff house. "If that's the case, then that would make this structure some sort of transporting device."

"A depot," Daniel said.

We turned to him.

"Like a train depot."

Andi slowly nodded. "Like a train depot. A place that connects universes."

"Well, whatever it was," Cowboy said, "I'm sure glad we're out of it."

"We're not." The professor motioned back to the beach and sea beyond . . . or what had been the beach and sea. Like the hallway we had just left, it was melting. And behind the melting something else was forming. Tall, huge and spreading toward us. With people, thousands of them. They sat in bleachers that kept multiplying, growing taller and taller. And with the people came the sound of cheering.

"Is that . . ." I blinked, trying to understand the impossible.

Cowboy helped out: " . . . a stadium."

The professor turned and started up the steps to the front door.

"What are you doing?" I called.

He nodded back to the melting sand and the growing stadium behind it. "I have no intention of waiting here."

He knocked on the wooden door. There was no answer. He knocked harder. The melting sand was getting closer. So was the stadium behind it. And the roar of the crowd. He was about to bang again when the door suddenly opened. And there stood the old nun, as bright and cheery as ever.

She opened the door wider and the professor barged in without a word. Unfazed, she stood there smiling, waiting for the rest of us. Daniel grabbed my hand and pulled me up the steps. We hurried through the door followed by Andi and Cowboy.

Inside, the entry hall was exactly the same. Same bureau and mirror, same coat tree, grandfather clock, fancy stairs with polished wood. The nun stepped to the same double doors, opened them and motioned us into the same living room.

"She gonna lock us inside again?" Cowboy asked.

"Most likely," the professor said.

I glanced over my shoulder. The stadium had just finished building and towered over our heads. But the melting sand kept coming. It had reached the bottom of the steps and was beginning to dissolve them.

"Considering the alternatives," Andi said, "it's probably best we enter."

The professor grunted and stepped into the living room along with the rest of us. Everything was back to normal, if that's the right word. Same stone walls, same pictures, same Victorian furniture.

The nun reached for the double doors and started to close them when the professor blocked her. "Must you?" he asked.

She smiled and motioned back to the entry hall. The melting had reached the front door. The professor sighed and let her close the doors. A quiet click followed.

"Now what?" I said.

"I reckon we should get as far away from this side of the room as possible," Cowboy said.

We hurried across the living room to the opposite door–the one Cowboy had destroyed, but was now in perfect condition.

"We just can't keep doing this," I said.

The professor was catching his breath. "You have an annoying habit of stating the obvious."

Across the room, the double doors had started to melt. So had the walls and furniture closest to them. And growing up just a few feet behind them? Not the bright oak paneling. Not all those desks and computer monitors. Instead, some sort of training room was sprouting. It had lots of tables and giant, monster-looking men lying on them. Only one guy looked normal. He was standing, working over the others like some kind of doctor or trainer or something. And he looked exactly like—

"Tank?" Andi gasped. She took a half step closer to see, then turned back to Cowboy. "Is that you?"

Cowboy could only stare. We all did.

"This is much too unusual," the professor said.

I shot him a look. "Now, who's stating the obvious?"

The melting floor kept coming. The professor opened the door. There was the hall with the back stairway, the dining room and kitchen just like before. And just like the house in Washington.

"What do we do now?" Andi asked.

"The catacomb," the professor said. "In the Capuchin Crypt." He turned to me. "You took photographs of the floor plan with your cell phone."

I pulled the phone from my pocket and flipped through the photos.

"Andrea, you said the bone pattern on the wall was identical to the floor plan of the house in Washington."

"Precisely. Other than the double doors sealing off the entry hall, they are identical."

I found the photos and enlarged one.

She pointed to it. "See. There's the entry hall with the formal stairway. Here's the living room we just crossed through. The hallway we're currently standing in, the back stairs, the dining room, and . . . what's this?" She pointed to a knuckle bone or something in the middle of the kitchen. It was slightly darker than the others, almost red.

The professor looked a moment then quietly answered. "The feast is in the kitchen."

We turned to him.

"That is what Hartmann said about the spear."

"The taxi driver, too," Cowboy said.

I glanced over to the door. It had started melting.

"Do you suppose . . ." Andi looked down the hallway toward the kitchen.

The professor repeated, "The feast is in the kitchen." He turned and started down the hall. We traded looks as he said it again, louder. "The feast is in the kitchen."

Without a word we followed.

Chapter 9

"I don't see nothin'," Cowboy said. "It's just a kitchen."

And he was right. Fancier than mine (its cupboards actually had food), but nothing special. Sink, stove, fridge. A little eating area to the side. There was an island in the center, but nothing to write home about.

"What did you expect," the professor said as he opened the fridge, "a sign reading, 'Look here for the spear that pierced Christ's side?'" He began rifling through the usual suspects and tossing them on the ground—milk, bread, eggs. "Don't just stand there, people. Search!"

We moved to action. Andi and Cowboy took one side of the kitchen with its cupboards and drawers, me and Daniel took the other. I looked behind the plates and glasses. Taking the professor's cue, I swept them off their shelves letting them crash to the floor. No one bothered looking down the hallway. We knew what was coming.

"Alrightee!" Cowboy shouted. "Hold up. Hold up, I said! Ain't no need lookin' further. I found it."

We turned to see him holding an old piece of metal—five, six inches long, with some wood attached. I'm guessing it was the head of the spear. Well, half of it anyway. The thing had been cut long ways, right down the middle.

I stepped closer to look.

"That's far enough," he said. "No need for you to come closer."

"I'm just taking a look at—"

"Stop, I said! Stop right there!"

I slowed to a stop and frowned.

"This is mine! I found it fair and square. And no matter how you try, there's no one gonna take it from me, you got that?"

I traded looks with the others. The good ol' boy accent was the same, but the charm was gone. "What's goin' on, Cowboy?"

"My name's not Cowboy." He turned to Andi and the professor. "And it ain't Tank, either. "It's Bjorn Hutton Christensen . . . the third."

"Yeah," I said, "very impressive." I started toward him again. "So why you gettin' all hot and—"

"Ah-ha!" Andi cried.

I turned to see her pull what looked like the other

half of the spear from the back of a utensil drawer. You couldn't miss the look of triumph on her face.

Or the anger on Cowboy's. "That's mine," he shouted. "It belongs with this one here."

Andi shook her head. "Wrong. Your piece belongs with mine."

The professor and I glanced at each other.

Cowboy broke into his smile and took a step toward her. "No big deal. I'm sure we can work it out. For starters, why don't you be a good little girl and just hand that over—"

"It's mine!" She yanked her piece to her chest. "It's in my possession and you can't have it."

"Yeah?" he said. "Just watch me."

He started at her until the professor stepped between them. "This is hardly the time to quibble over—"

"It's mine!" Andi pulled away. "I found it and by all rights, his piece should also—"

"I found mine first! That half belongs to me!"

"And that?" The professor pointed to the melting floor just coming into the kitchen. "Who would like possession of that?"

"I can stop it," Andi said. "If he gives me my other half, I'll have more than enough power to stop it."

"*Your* half?" Cowboy shoved the professor aside and started for her. "You give me *my* half!"

"Stop it!" I shouted. "Cowboy!"

But Andi didn't need my help. She squared off to face the big guy, holding up her piece like a weapon. "My intelligence is greater than yours. I can manage this power far more wisely than some ignorant farm boy."

Cowboy slowed and sneered. "You think you're so

smart with your brains and all. Well brains got nothin' over real strength. Not when it comes to—"

"Look!" I pointed at the melting floor closing in.

Cowboy started at her again. "It needs strength. Not some brainiac with—"

"Stay back!" Andi crouched, ready to spring. "You've been warned!"

He laughed, then lunged at her. She screamed as he grabbed her arm. But he was too focused on getting the weapon to see her knee come up sharp and hard.

It found its mark. He was more startled than hurt. She used that split second of surprise to pull his hand into her chest, bringing his piece next to hers.

There was no flash, no sound. Just a look that came into her eyes. Wild, full of wonder.

Cowboy saw it, too. He blinked. Surprised at his actions. Surprised at hers. "Andi?"

She yanked the metal out of his hand and pulled away. Now she had both pieces, clutching them, hunching over them like some crazed animal.

"Andi?" Cowboy reached for her. Not the spear. Her.

She looked up at him. She smiled. Then she threw herself at him—shoving him backwards. Not much, but enough. His left heel caught the edge of the melting floor. He tried pulling it away, but it had him. It quickly ran up his foot and turned it into liquid. Then his ankle. Then his leg.

He looked down at it, puzzled. Then to us. There was no pain on his face. Just confusion. The melting spread up to his knee, his thigh. And, as it melted, he sank.

By the time I got to him the liquid had reached his

other foot and started melting his other leg, sinking him into the floor. I reached down to him—the liquid just inches from my own feet. "My hand!" I shouted. "Take my hand!"

He saw the floor coming at me, knew the danger.

"Take my hand!"

He looked back up. Now he was up to his waist.

"Take my hand!"

But he wouldn't.

I took half a step back, the floor nearly touching the toe of my shoes. But I kept reaching, arching my back, trying to stay clear. "Take my hand!"

He'd melted up to his chest.

"No, Miss Brenda."

"Cowboy!"

He kept sinking until he was up to his neck. Only his head was above the floor, more than a little creepy.

I stretched with all I had. That's when I lost my balance. I swore and fell . . . until the professor swooped in and grabbed my waist. He yanked me back so hard we tumbled onto the solid floor.

When I scrambled to my hands and knees Cowboy was gone.

Chapter 13

I leapt to my feet and spun around to Andi shouting, "What have you done?"

She stared, as surprised as the rest of us. But there was no missing the awe on her face and in her voice. "The power . . . don't you see it?" She motioned to the floor. It melted at the regular speed but the area closest to her had slowed. It was circling, going around her. "I can feel it. Energy is flowing through me."

We watched as she put the two pieces of metal into one hand and raised it high over her head. "I order you to stop!" she shouted.

It didn't. Not completely. But the melting had definitely slowed. She was standing close to the island

and all three of us edged next to her.

"That's right," she said. "Good. There's no need to be afraid. Come closer. I'll protect you."

Nobody was crazy about the idea. But nobody liked what happened to Cowboy, either.

She turned back to the floor and shouted, "By the authority granted to me, I order you to stop!"

It may have slowed some more, but it kept inching forward. We backed up until we were pressed against the island.

"I command you to stop!"

"It won't," Daniel said quietly. I looked at him. "It's purer than her."

"Purer?" the professor said.

Daniel nodded then hopped up on the kitchen island.

"What are you doing?" Andi said. "I have the spear, the one that killed Christ."

Daniel motioned for me to join him. With the melting floor just feet away it seemed a good idea.

Andi tried again. "I order you to halt!"

Still no luck.

The professor decided to join us. It took a little effort with his old bones, but we got him up on the counter, too.

By now the whole kitchen was pretty melted—cupboards, sink, frig – everything but the shrinking circle around Andi and our island.

"Andrea, come up here," the professor ordered. "Join us."

"But . . ." She looked back at the floor. It was inches from her feet.

"Get up here. Now!"

She had no choice and finally hopped up on the

island.

The last of the floor quickly melted. Now all four of us sat there. A little boat in an ocean of a melting kitchen.

But the boat was also melting. It shifted, then dropped half a foot. We pulled in our feet, scrambled up until we were standing. It slumped again, hard. So hard we could barely keep our balance. Like an ice cube on a griddle, the whole thing kept getting smaller and smaller.

It lunged to the left, throwing all of us off balance. The professor the worst.

"No!" he cried.

His feet slipped until they touched the liquid. Me and Daniel grabbed his hands, but we were too late. It washed over his feet, dissolving them as fast as they had Cowboy.

"Let go!" he shouted.

We wouldn't.

It rose to his ankles, his calves.

"I order you to release me!"

"Shut up!" I yelled.

He fought us, trying to break free as he kept sinking . . . up to his thighs, his hips.

"Release me or you'll also perish!"

"I said shut up!"

He was up to his chest.

We wouldn't let go.

But the professor had other ideas. He twisted until he wrenched both hands free.

"NO!" I yelled.

He threw himself backwards.

"Professor!"

He didn't scream. He didn't shout. There was a

brief second as the back of his head lay on the surface then sank, followed by his face. Now there was only his flailing arms and hands until they also disappeared.

"Professor!"

The island was three feet off the floor. It pitched so hard me and Daniel could barely stay on top.

Andi wasn't so lucky. "Help me!" she screamed as she fell.

She sank like a stone, throwing out her arms, holding the spear high over her head as the floor swallowed her . . . but not before Daniel lunged forward and grabbed it.

Even that didn't help. The last of our little island was quickly melting. I grabbed Daniel and hoisted him onto my hip . . . just as the floor swept over my feet. There was no pain. Just a warmth. It kept rising, absorbing my legs, my thighs.

Daniel scampered higher—clinging to my neck with one hand, holding the spear with the other. I felt the warmth wash around my belly, rising to my chest. I helped him up onto my shoulders.

A moment later I saw it touch his feet. He didn't cry out, just lifted the spear high over his head. The floor surrounded my neck now. I lifted my head to breathe. One gulp of air, two—before it rose over my mouth and nose. And then I was gone.

Chapter 11

It was like a dream.

But it wasn't.

The art studio. The dozen or so kids at their easels. I'd never been here, but I'd also spent years teaching in this very classroom . . . and loving every minute of it.

They were special needs children—Garret, the Asian kid with MS, Lucy sitting in her wheel chair in the final stages of leukemia, sweet Melissa with her severe learning disabilities. I knew them all . . . yet I'd never met them.

"That's good," I said to Rupert, his genetic

disorder so severe he could only paint with a brush between his clenched teeth. The canvas was smeared in blacks and browns. "What would happen if you put a splash of red in there? Maybe even yellow?"

He looked up at me, his eyes beaming. And my heart melted.

That's why I do what I do. Art therapy. Letting these kids express themselves when nobody else will listen. This month it's paint. Next month it'll be clay. Anything to give them an outlet . . . and to take their minds off the ugliness of the world destruction.

"World destruction?" The phrase surprised me. I looked around the room for a window. It was the same dimension as the living room in the cliff house, the one I'd spent so much time dreaming about.

Or was this the dream?

But it wasn't a living room. It was a classroom. Bright lights, cheery colors, rainbows and animals painted on the walls.

I found a window and crossed to it. The shutters were closed.

"Miss Brenda, Miss Brenda, come see what I've done." It was Lindsey, an eight-year-old who had been abandoned at the church by her parents. There was a lot of that now. With the plague, the famine, and the war—parents were unable to care for their children, particularly those with special needs.

I stopped. Were such things true? They hadn't been before.

"Miss Brenda?"

"I'll be right there, kiddo." I pushed open the shutters. We were in a big city, crowded, buildings packed super tight. Three stories below on the sidewalk people wore face masks. Like in a hospital.

Some even had gas masks. And for good reason. The air was a thick, puke-green.

I stared, trying to understand . . . until someone touched my sleeve.

I turned. It was Daniel. Littlefoot was beside him. I knelt in front of them, remembering the other dream, the one in the melting kitchen. "What are you doing here? You all right? Where are the others?"

He shook his head.

"What?" I said.

"Gone."

I searched his face. "Andi? Cowboy? The professor?" I knew the names, but not from here.

"All dead."

"When? How?"

He pointed out the window.

"I don't understand."

"Everyone dies."

"But—"

"In this world everyone dies."

"In this . . ." my mind spun, trying to fit the pieces, remembering what Andi had said about a multiverse "In this world, in this . . . *universe?*"

He nodded.

"Everyone will die in *this* universe?"

"Yes," he said.

"But in the other—Cowboy and the others, they won't die? This—" I turned to the window, "this won't happen?"

"If you come back and help."

I rose and looked around the classroom. "But this . . . this is my life. This has always been my life."

"No."

He was right of course. The other world had been

too real.

"This is what makes me happy."

He shook his head and pointed out the window.

"What?"

His voice filled with emotion. "We can stop this."

"If we go back?" I said. "If we go back to our other world?"

"Yes."

I looked to Littlefoot. Her eyes had shifted colors. Now they were a deep, cobalt blue. She reached out her hand to me. I stared at it then turned back to Daniel. He looked more serious than I'd ever seen him.

I turned back to the girl. She nodded, did her best to smile. Daniel gently reached for my hand, took it, and placed it in hers.

I didn't pull it away.

Without a word she turned and we threaded our way through the classroom. Daniel followed. One by one the children stopped painting. They turned and stared. More like glared. But not at me. At Daniel and the girl.

"Miss Brenda . . .?" It was Lindsey. "Are you okay? Are they hurting you?"

"What?" I smiled. "No, of course not, we're just old friends."

She didn't look convinced. Neither did the others.

I leaned down to Daniel and whispered, "What's going on?"

He motioned to Littlefoot and himself. "We don't belong."

"What?"

"It's not our universe."

"But it's mine?"

"Only if you want."

We continued around the artwork and the kids that I loved so dearly. When we arrived at the double doors they opened as if by magic and there stood the roly-poly nun with the perma-smile.

I stepped into the entry hall.

"Miss Brenda?" It was Lindsey again.

I turned and called, "Don't worry, sweetheart. I'll be fine."

Littlefoot reached for the front door.

"Wait." I turned to Daniel. "If I leave, can I return?"

He held my gaze and slowly shook his head.

I turned back to the classroom. There was such joy here. Such . . . purpose. "I love this place," I said. "And these kids. They're my life."

The moisture welling up in Daniel's eyes said he understood. "It will be better," he said. "If you come with us, *they* will be better."

I stared into those deep brown eyes. There was no missing their sincerity. He'd never lied to me before. I glanced up to the nun who stood beside him. She gave a nod of silent assurance. I looked back into the room, the children, my life's work . . . and slowly returned the nod.

The nun gently closed the double doors. I turned to face the girl. She reached for the front door, opened it, and we stepped outside.

Chapter 12

Our feet had barely touched the stone steps before Littlefoot turned around and knocked on the door again.

The nun answered, beamed like she hadn't seen us in forever, and ushered us inside. But when Sister of the Perpetual Smiles opened the double doors to my classroom, things were completely different.

Instead of kids with easels, there were all those desks that I'd seen before—back when we were running from the melting floor the first time. Same light, oak paneling, same computer monitors manned by the same computer geeks. Everything the same, except . . .

Near the end of the room, on a raised platform, behind an expensive desk sat . . .

"Andi?" I shouted.

She looked up, along with the rest of the room. I raced to her—not running, but not exactly walking, either. The two kids followed.

When we got there she was already standing, taking off her glasses. "Do I know—"

"It's Brenda."

She frowned. "I . . . I dreamt about you. Just last night. And the night before." Her frown deepened. "But . . . we've never met. Have we?"

"Of course we've met. We've been together all day. And a few months on top of that."

"I'm sorry, I—"

"In the other universe. *Our* universe."

"I beg your pardon?"

"The multiverse thing."

"Multiverse? But that's . . . just theory."

"You tell that to the melting floor and everything else happening to us."

Her eyes widened. "It wasn't a dream? It *was* you." She looked at Daniel and Littlefoot. "And you. I saw you, too."

"The professor," I said, "is he here?"

"The professor. He was with us too, wasn't he?"

"Yeah, yeah. Is he with you?"

She hesitated. I looked out over the room. By now every computer jockey was staring at us. And they weren't exactly smiling. "Who are these guys?" I said.

"What? Oh, they're my employees. This is an information and research facility."

"Not very friendly."

"Yes." She put on her glasses for a better look. "I don't understand. They're normally quite congenial."

"They don't want us here," I said.

She looked at me.

"And trust me, the feeling's mutual. Get the professor and let's go."

She scowled and looked over to the far wall.

"So is he here or not?"

She stepped off the platform and started across the room. I traded looks with the kids and followed—the geeks watching our every move. When I caught up to her I said, "Daniel and his girlfriend here say we got to get back to our own universe. So let's find the professor and get our butts outta—"

We'd reached the opposite wall and she pointed to it. "What?" I said.

She motioned to a small drawer built into the wall. A brass plaque was on it.

I leaned in and squinted to read:

Dr. James McKinney 1955-2013.

I turned to her. "The professor, he's—"

She nodded. "Several years ago.

"And that's him? In there?"

"His ashes, yes. He asked to be interned here. It may interest you to know that this entire center is named in his honor."

"But he's not dead. Not in the other universe. Not in ours."

"This *is* my universe. This is what we lived for. What he . . . died for."

I looked out over the angry faces and gave a snort.

"You have no idea what joy I have here," she said. "The thrill of all of this information right at my fingertips. Anything and everything. It's a dream come true."

"And the rest of the world?"

"You mean the riots? The radiation poisoning?"

"Riots? There aren't any riots."

She frowned.

"Yeah, well, maybe in this universe," I said. "Whatever they got going here, I'm betting it's pretty ugly. But the thing is, you and me, all of us, there's a chance we can change it. If we go back we can fix things so they—"

"That's extremely doubtful."

It was my turn to frown.

She lowered her voice to a whisper. "The odds of us, of anybody, overthrowing The Gate are extremely—"

"I'm sorry, did you say, 'The Gate?'"

She motioned me to lower my voice.

I continued, "They're the ones we're suppose to keep the spear from. Remember the Cardinal? That was our whole purpose. To get the spear before the Gate did."

She glanced around, afraid someone would hear.

"Look, we're in the middle of something here. I don't know what, but it looks like we're a team or something. All of us." I motioned to the drawer. "And the professor, if we go back, he'll still be alive."

She stood a moment looking at the plaque.

"Trust me, the jerk is still alive. You saw him an hour ago. You dreamed 'bout him. About us."

She shook her head. "No."

"Of course you did. You—"

"No. It was not a dream." She grew more confident. "It was an alternate reality. The multiverse." She turned toward the double doors across the room. "And if this structure is indeed a portal—" She looked to Daniel. "Or as you've stated, 'a depot,' it should be fairly simple to return." She started forward.

The kids and I traded looks. She was in.

We followed her across the room. The geeks were getting out of their seats. One or two tried intimidating us by flexing their geek bodies. Good luck with that.

We were practically there when Andi slowed. "But Tank? Where is Tank?"

"He's not here with you?"

"No."

I swore.

Then her face brightened. "The training room!"

"What?"

"The room we saw next to the stadium, do you remember it?"

"Yeah, but—"

She crossed to the double doors and opened them. There, waiting in the entry hall was, who else, but Sister Smiles. The old lady motioned us forward and we stepped in. Littlefoot reached behind us to shut the double doors. Andi touched her shoulder and she stopped just long enough for Andi to look out over the room one last time.

Then, taking a breath for courage, she turned and nodded to the nun. The woman opened the front door and we stepped outside.

Actually, inside.

The door opened to the entrance of the giant stadium we'd seen before. They were playing football. Well, a type of football.

Chapter 13

For starters, every lineman had some sort of club, or battle ax or something. Like those old Gladiator movies. Only these guys were monsters. Literally. Five, six hundred pounds apiece. Real knuckle draggers.

I turned to Andi and shouted the obvious, "Steroids?"

"Perhaps. More likely, genetic manipulation. In fact, if you notice the ratio of height to weight you can see a reoccurring pattern of—"

A play began and she was drowned out by the roar of the crowd. Each team went at the other—grunting, shouting, clubbing, hacking. And blood. Lots of it. The quarterback got sacked. And for good measure they started bludgeoning him to death.

The crowd cheered.

Andi leaned over and puked.

"See any sign of Tank?" I shouted.

She shook her head. So did Daniel and the girl.

Andi looked back up and groaned, "Oh no."

I followed her gaze to the field. The monster boys on the sidelines were turning toward us.

"What's the deal?" I shouted. "What are they looking at?" But I already knew. So did Andi. And it wasn't just the players. The fans were also turning toward us.

"They know we don't belong," Andi said. "They sense it."

"We got as much right bein' here as them."

She looked around. "You may think so and I may think so . . ." She nodded toward the dozen Neanderthals leaving their bench and lumbering up the steps toward us. "But they don't."

"Any suggestions?"

"Just one."

She looked at me. I looked at her. We spun around to the cliff behind us and began banging on the wooden door.

Sister Happy Face took her sweet time to answer, so I threw in a little R rated language to speed up the process. By the time she opened the door the goon squad was a dozen yards behind us. We ran into the entry hall and she slammed the door a second before they arrived with their own version of banging and cussing.

Daniel pushed open the double doors to the living room. Only now it was the training room. A handful of the big bruisers were stretched out on the tables groaning and moaning. Some were bleeding. All were waited on by the one and only—

"Tank!" Andi rushed to him.

The big fella barely had time to look up before she threw her arms around him. He returned the hug, more than a little awkward. When she stepped back, she pulled herself together, even more awkward.

He broke into that big-hearted grin of his. "Andi."

"You remember."

"Remember? Shucks, I dream about you all the time! I mean, that is to say, well not all the time, but what I mean is . . . It's you! You're real!" He spotted me and the kids and broke into an even bigger grin. "You're *all* real!" He reached out his arms to Littlefoot and she ran into them for a hug. "It's sure swell to see you again!"

She looked up to him and grinned back, those blue eyes now liquid brown.

The goon lying on the table in front of him groaned. Probably because of the bone sticking out of his arm.

"Oh, sorry, partner." Cowboy reached down and wrapped both of his hands around the arm. He closed his eyes and began silently moving his lips. Just like old times.

Meanwhile the bruisers kept banging on the front door until you could actually hear the wood planks starting to crack.

When Cowboy pulled away his hands the arm was as good as new. Not even scar tissue.

"That's what you do here?" I said.

"Yeah." He shot me his good ol' boy grin. "It's pretty fun. And I get to make lots of new friends." He turned to the guy on the table. "Ain't that right, Gus?"

Gus moved his arm, grunted and showed his appreciation by lunging for Andi.

She screamed and jumped back.

Cowboy slammed him back down on the table. "Come on, now. That's no way to treat our guests."

Gus groaned. Too weak to try again. But he wasn't the only one with an attitude. The whole room was turning and staring. Several even managed to growl.

"What's wrong, fellas?" Cowboy called. "These here, they're my pals."

"We don't belong," I explained. "We're in the wrong dimension."

"Universe," Andi corrected. "We're in the wrong multiverse and they sense it."

The front door was beginning to splinter.

"We gotta get outa here." I said.

"Brenda's right." Andi grabbed Cowboy's hand and tried pulling him toward the hallway. But he wouldn't budge.

"These . . . are my friends."

"Maybe your friends," I said, "but not ours. Look how much they hate us."

Gus made my point by sitting up and lunging for me. He was stronger than before and it took more effort for Cowboy to shove him back down. "But I help these guys," he said. "Me and the Lord, we fix 'em up. And I really like it. I like it a whole bunch."

Some of the goons from the other tables were struggling to their feet.

"We know you do," Andi said. "And that's very commendable. But there's something even greater."

"Greater than this?"

"You can make things better," I said. "*We* can make things better. But you gotta come back with us."

The bruisers who'd made it to their feet began hobbling toward us. It was like a scene from *The Walking Dead*.

Andi quickly explained. "In this reality, you're only a band aid, you're only fixing something that's already broken. If we go back, there's a chance we can prevent the multiverse from splitting like this; there's a chance we can stop all this from happening before it begins."

"She's right," I said. "We can do it. If we roll up our sleeves and all work together, we can do it!" I winced at my cheesiness, not really sure I believed it.

But Cowboy did. He looked from me to Andi. Then he looked to Littlefoot, who was nodding. He turned back to Andi and she reached for his hand again. This time he took it . . . just as the front door exploded open.

We turned and ran. Gus, the goon, caught my jacket but I spun around and slipped out of it—a parting gift.

When we got to the hallway I glanced over my shoulder. The players from the stadium had joined those in the training room.

"The stairs!" Cowboy shouted.

It made sense. No way was I goin' back into that kitchen. I grabbed Daniel's hand, he grabbed the girl's, and we raced up the steps. We were halfway to the top when the whole staircase began to shake—no doubt from the extra tons of muscle that had just started up them.

We made it to the top and Andi started for the first bedroom door. The one we'd escaped through before. But this time it wasn't real. Just a painting of a door.

She ran to the second. This one was real and she threw it open.

We gasped. And for good reason. There was another me lying there on a bed, passed out with a needle jammed in my arm.

"What?" I cried. "That's not possible."

"It's your nightmare," Andi said. "Up in Washington. It's the universe where you had the overdose."

I tried to step in for a closer look but she pulled me back. "No," she said. "It's a paradox!"

"A what?"

"A time paradox." She pushed us out and slammed the door shut behind her. "It's too dangerous!"

"Not as dangerous as these boys." Cowboy pointed to the players who'd reached the top of the stairs.

We ran to the next door and tried it. It was locked. I slammed into it with my shoulder.

"Let me!" Cowboy stepped in and hit it once, twice. It took three hits before the lock broke and it opened. But instead of the door flying open and into the room, it flew out at us . . . pushed by a thousand gallons of water that roared over us, slamming us to the ground and rolling us down the hall.

It drained in seconds and we made it to our feet, gagging and coughing up sea water.

I shouted to Andi. "That was *your* nightmare, where you were drowning."

"Yes!"

The flood slowed the bruisers behind us, but not by much. They were already clamoring to their feet and stumbling toward us.

The main stairway with the fancy banister was just ahead. The perfect escape—down the steps, through the entry hall and out to the beach or whatever would be there. There was only one problem.

Players were also coming up them.

"Now what?" Cowboy shouted. "We're surrounded."

Daniel raised his arm and pointed to a closed door at the very end of the hall. Not a door to a room at the end of the hall, but simply a door at the end of the hall—as in, open it, step out and fall out of the house. It hadn't been there until now. I was sure of it. I was also sure I recognized it from Washington. But there, the door was on the first floor and it led into a basement with some pretty ugly stuff.

One other thing. Sister Smiles was standing beside it. But instead of motioning us toward it, she was motioning us to get down on the floor.

It made no sense. But it didn't matter to Daniel. He dropped to the ground, digging his hands into the carpet a fraction of a second before she opened the door and all hell broke lose. I'm not swearing. It *was* hell, complete with the red glow and leaping flames.

There was also wind. Lots of it. But, unlike the last door, nothing was racing out at us. Instead, we were being sucked toward it. It pulled on my clothes, my hair. My whole body was being dragged toward it. I dropped to my knees, grabbed the only thing I could find–some door molding—and hung on with just my finger tips.

"Look out!" Cowboy yelled.

I turned and ducked just as the first of the big boys tumbled past. I flattened myself against the wall as another rolled by. And then another. And another. Until there was a steady stream of bodies being sucked into the doorway.

My fingertips ached. Any minute they'd give out. I turned to Daniel. He was slipping, losing his grip on the carpet.

"Hang on!" I shouted.

He dug in, but the wind was too strong.

"Grab my leg!"

He looked at me.

"Grab my leg!"

Finally, his grip failed. He slid past and just barely caught my ankle in time.

My fingers cramped, on fire, but I yelled, "We'll be okay! Hang on!"

He knew I was lying. He knew my fingers were giving way. I saw it in his eyes. And I saw something else, too.

"No!" I shouted. "Don't!"

He started to smile.

"Daniel! No!"

It was that sad, crooked smile.

"No! Don't you dare let go! Don't you—"

But he did let go. He fell away without a sound.

"DANIEL . . ."

He was gone. Bodies kept flying past, but he was gone. I cried out. A scream. It came from deep down in my gut. I couldn't breathe. It was over. There was nothing left. My fingers gave way or I let go, it didn't matter. The wind dragged me across the carpet. I started to tumble, to roll. It didn't matter.

Until something grabbed my arm.

I looked up to see Cowboy grinning down at me. "Just hang on, Miss Brenda!"

He began to pull.

"Daniel . . ." I shouted. "Daniel's—"

"Just hang on." Somehow he'd wedged his body into the last bedroom doorway where he braced himself as he kept pulling. I saw the strain on his face, the pain. And the impossibility.

"Let go!" I shouted. "Let me go!"

But he didn't. He wouldn't. He kept pulling . . . until he finally dragged me out of the hall and we tumbled into the room . . . with Andi and —

"Daniel!" I cried.

He grinned and giggled as I crawled to him, as Andi and Cowboy fought to close the door.

I pulled him into me. Holding him, kissing the top of his head. I couldn't get enough. And when we finally parted, I did it all over again.

Chapter 14

Cowboy leaned his head against the closed door, catching his breath, as the last of the wind died. He got to his feet and looked around the room, breaking into that big grin of his. "Don't you just love this place?"

"Love" wasn't exactly my word of first choice . . . or my last. But if the pattern of the Washington house was true, this is where he had his God encounter. Either way I was glad we were safe. Daniel looked just fine. So did Andi. But the girl . . .

"Where's Littlefoot?" I asked.

Cowboy's grin faded. He looked down and took a deep breath. And then another.

Andi answered for him. "She never made it."

I nodded and got to my feet. I wasn't sure what to say or do. Daniel saved me the trouble. He reached for the door.

"No, don't!" Andi cried. "We're not sure—"

Too late. He'd opened it. And three feet away, standing on the beach, in all his stuffy-butt glory, was . . .

"Professor!" Andi threw herself at him, all hugs and tears. "You're alive!"

He endured the emotion and did his best to return it. "Do you have the slightest idea how long I have been waiting? Andrea, please!"

She wiped her eyes as the rest of us stepped outside to join them.

He motioned to the front door of the house which, just a moment ago, had been the door to the bedroom. "I have been outside, knocking upon this blasted door for half an hour. Would you mind telling me why you took so long to answer?"

I shrugged. "Long story."

"Well, I expect to hear every detail. And the spear?"

We traded looks.

"Don't tell me you failed to retrieve it? After all we've been through?"

More looks.

"We could go back," Cowboy said. He turned to the door. "I bet that nice nun would—"

"No," the professor said. "I believe we've endured

quite enough, thank you very much. We shall return to the Vatican and tell Hartmann that his wild goose chase has come to—"

He stopped as Daniel pulled both halves of the spearhead from his back pocket.

I blinked. I'm betting we all did.

"That's fantastic!" Andi cried. "Great job, Daniel." She reached for the spear, but the professor quickly stepped between them.

"No."

She turned to him.

"From your past behavior, that is an unwise decision." He eyed Daniel suspiciously. "How are you feeling, son? Any unusual emotions? Thoughts of grandeur? A desire for control?"

Daniel shook his head.

"Very well. Then I suggest it remain in your possession until it is delivered."

We agreed and Daniel slipped it back into his pocket.

Without a word, the professor turned and started up the beach.

Professor?" Andi called. "Where are you going?"

"Why to the taxi, of course."

"He's back?"

"The man claims his 'voice' told him to return; though I suspect the voice was more concerned in the profit of a running meter than in any humanitarian effort."

"Wait," Cowboy said. "Hold on a moment." He turned back to the house "Shouldn't we tell that nice old lady how much we . . ."

He slowed to a stop. And for good reason.

There was no noise, no sound. But the house was

rising. Not the cliff. Just the house. At least the front of it. The door, the windows. They weren't solid anymore. They were clear, transparent. Like a cellophane wrapper slipping up and off the cliff, higher and higher.

"Everybody's seeing this, right?" Andi asked.

No one bothered to answer.

It cleared the top of the cliff, paused, then shot up into the sky. So fast it was a blur. One minute there. The next gone. Now there was only the rocky cliff.

I stepped up to where the door had been. Felt for it. There was nothing but smooth, cold stone. I stood back for a better look. There were hollows and ridges here and there that could of passed for windows. But that's all they were, hollows and ridges. It was just a rocky cliff.

Epilogue

The sun was setting by the time the taxi got us back to the Vatican. And it was just like old times . . .

- The professor browbeating another receptionist who said we couldn't see Cardinal Hartmann.
- The receptionist running off to his superiors (with or without tears, I couldn't tell from where I sat).
- Us sneaking through the little door and up to Hartmann's

apartment.
- Me knocking on the door.
- And the frail old assistant with the dirty Coke bottle glasses answering.

But Hartmann wasn't in. His blue velvet chair with the peeling gold paint sat in the middle of the room just like before, but that was it. Nothing else. 'Cept the memory of the sketch I made before we ever met. The one of the empty chair without him in it.

"When do you expect his return?" the professor asked.

The assistant thought a second, then raised a bony finger like he suddenly remembered something. He turned and shuffled to the old desk. We waited as he opened the drawer and pulled out an envelope. We waited even longer as he shuffled back to us.

He handed the envelope to the professor who turned it over. It had a red, waxed seal on the back. He opened it, pulled out a card and silently read.

We stood.

He re-read.

We shifted.

More re-reading.

The assistant took off his glasses and cleaned away a few layers of dust.

"Well?" I said.

The professor looked up . . . a lot paler than when he'd looked down. "He won't be able to see us."

"You tellin' me we go to all this trouble and he doesn't care enough to—"

"He wants us to leave the spear with his assistant."

We turned to the old timer who stopped polishing

his glasses and gave a silent, humble nod.

"Are you certain?" Andi said. "Do we really want to entrust something of this value and with this much power to—"

The professor ignored her and turned to Daniel. "Give it to him."

"Professor?"

"Now. Give it to him now."

Daniel nodded and pulled the two pieces of spear out of his back pocket. He handed them to the old timer who took them in both hands and gave another one of those humble nods.

When he looked up, he was smiling. Something else, too. It was probably just the light in the room, but I swear the color of his eyes had changed. Just like the girl's. They'd been a cloudy, cataract gray. Now they were a brilliant, sapphire blue.

The professor turned toward the door. "Let us go."

"What?" I said. "Just like that?"

"We've completed our task. Now it's time to leave. And do so quickly."

The assistant gave another smile and nodded like it was a good idea. He opened the door and we left. We wound through the halls and down the stairs pretty fast. But not fast enough.

We just got to the first floor and were heading for some giant brass doors when we heard, "You there. Stop."

The professor picked up his pace. We all did.

"Stop, I say."

Other priests and what-nots turned to stare at us. A guard appeared at the door. We slowed to a stop. Busted.

Some overfed priest waddled toward us with the receptionist.

"You wish to see Cardinal Hartmann?"

The professor turned and waited. He knew what was coming.

"Do you wish to see Cardinal Hartmann?"

"No," he sighed. "Not any more."

"And yet you came here—"

"It was a mistake," the professor said. "We didn't know."

"Know what?" I said.

The priest frowned like I had no business talking, much less breathing. I flipped my dreads to the side. "Know what?"

"Hartmann's dead," the professor said.

"He's what?"

"You are family?" the priest asked.

The professor shook his head. "Just friends."

"Please accept our sympathies. With the Lord he has been nearly six months now. Yet a day does not pass where he is not missed."

"No way," I said. "We were just with—"

The professor cut me off. "Yes. We did not know." Looking at me with meaning, he repeated. "We did not know." Before I could argue, he turned and headed through the doors and out into the courtyard.

I traded looks with the others and we followed.

The priest called after us. "We do miss him. All of us. His departure for us was a great loss."

I caught up to the professor. "What was that about?" He said nothing but kept walking. "Hey," I grabbed his arm. "What *was* that?"

He didn't slow. But he did answer. "That, Miss

Barnick, was a profound tragedy."

I scowled. "What?"

He swallowed hard. I watched as he covered his face with his hands, then lowered them to his mouth.

I softened. "You two were close."

"It's a far greater loss than losing a close friend." He slowed to a stop and we gathered around him. He looked at each of us. There was more than sadness in his eyes. There was fear. Anger. "I'm afraid the tragedy is ongoing. *Our* lives, each one of them, is set to unravel."

"What do you mean?" Andi asked.

He shook his head.

"Professor?"

He took a deep breath and resumed walking. "What's done is done," he said. "What's done is done and there is no turning it back."

Soli Deo gloria.

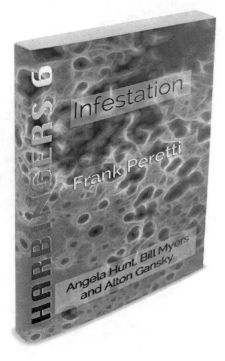

FROM HARBINGERS 6

INFESTATION

Frank Peretti

The teeming waters and the chatter-filled trees of the Indian River Lagoon put his mind at ease. He belonged here, wading waist deep through the shallows, peering through the tangled roots of the mangroves, feeling the sandy give of the sea bottom through his waders. His skiff followed close behind him, tethered by a rope around his waist. The short little box of a boat carried his camera, binoculars, notebook, and lunch. It also served as a quick resort should an alligator come too close - which so far had not been a problem. Alligators preferred the freshwater streams and culvert outlets, and those he'd seen in the lagoon were largely indifferent and safely distant.

All in keeping with the goodness of the day: the Florida sun, the alive-ness of the leaves and blooms, the constant flitter and flash of every color of bird, lizard, and fish in every direction.

Life. He was here to record and observe it, count and preserve it, and how he loved it.

He'd already spotted two manatee females with their calves, newborn this year, and four new pelican nests, three with eggs, one with hatchlings. Very good signs. At last, after so many mysterious deaths in this place - dolphins, manatees, pelicans - life was returning.

A ripple offshore alerted him. He reached for the skiff, drew it close. Alligators were stealthy and the lagoon was no place for inattention.

But ... no. A silvery gray dorsal fin broke the surface, a sight that made him grab his binoculars. He peered through the lenses, focused, anticipated the next breach -

The fin broke the surface again, dipped below, then broke again, this time with a puff of air and a gray arched back that glinted in the sun.

A dolphin!

He laughed in joy. How long had it been since he'd

seen a dolphin in this part of the lagoon? And where there was one, there were sure to be more. He scanned the placid waters, then set the binoculars in the skiff and watched.

The dolphin seemed to be alone, and now it was circling back, coming closer, a nice bit of luck. He might get a chance to judge the size, age, and health. Viral outbreaks among the dolphins in the past had made him and his fellow biologists careful to observe and record any anomalies - such as this particular dolphin's behavior: not playful or vigorous, but sluggish, and oddly single-minded. It was still coming his way on a straight course.

Cautious, he yanked the skiff in close and watched as the dolphin approached, then slowed and circled no more than ten feet away. It was an adult, average size. That it would come in so close suggested it might be habituated to humans and was either curious or expecting a handout.

But the sheen and color of the skin and the listless behavior looked all too familiar. This dolphin was ill, probably dying.

He chanced a very slow movement toward it.

Rather than shying away, it drifted closer.

Habituated. Had to be. No wild dolphin would act this friendly.

Standing next to it now, he observed a greenish tint on the skin, possibly an algae. The dolphin allowed a gentle brush of his hand; a green residue clouded the water.

He leaned close to check the eye—

The eye was gone, nothing but an empty socket oozing green.

"What the—"

The dolphin sidled closer and he could sense the rules of the encounter changing. Now the dolphin was pressing into his space and he was the one feeling timid. He fought off the feelings, reached to examine the flank—

His hand passed through the skin as if it were sodden newspaper. The flesh within felt like goo between his fingers. When he yanked his hand away, it was coated in green slime. A cloud of green billowed out of the dolphin's flank, fouling the water.

What was this? Another algae? Another plague of phytoplankton? He clambered in the skiff for a sample jar, dipped it into the green cloud ...

The dolphin rolled lazily onto its side. The movement drew his attention, he turned his head, looked into the wound his hand had made.

The wound tore open, green slime exploded into his face. All he saw was oozing, shimmering green.

And then nothing.

OTHER BOOKS BY BILL MYERS

NOVELS
Child's Play
The Judas Gospel
The God Hater
The Voice
Angel of Wrath
The Wager
Soul Tracker
The Presence
The Seeing
The Face of God
When the Last Leaf Falls
Eli
Blood of Heaven
Threshold
Fire of Heaven

NON-FICTION
The Jesus Experience—Journey Deeper into the Heart of God
Supernatural Love
Supernatural War

CHILDREN BOOKS
Baseball for Breakfast (picture book)
The Bug Parables (picture book series)
Bloodstone Chronicles (fantasy series)
McGee and Me (book/video series)
The Incredible Worlds of Wally McDoogle
   (comedy series)
Bloodhounds, Inc. (mystery series)
The Elijah Project (supernatural suspense series)

Secret Agent Dingledorf and His Trusty Dog Splat
   (comedy series)
TJ and the Time Stumblers (comedy series)
Truth Seekers (action adventure series)

TEEN BOOKS
Forbidden Doors (supernatural suspense)
   Dark Power Collection
   Invisible Terror Collection
   Deadly Loyalty Collection
   Ancient Forces Collection

For a complete list of Bill's books, sample chapters, and newsletter signup go to www.Billmyers.com Or check out his Facebook page: www.facebook.com/billmyersauthor.

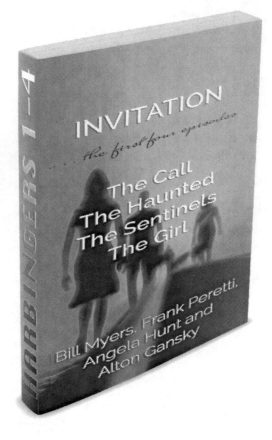

Now available:

Cycle One: Invitation

The first four books in one volume

If you enjoyed this book, please leave a review at your favorite online bookstore.

CPSIA information can be obtained at www.ICGtesting.com
Printed in the USA
LVOW10s2353270716

498073LV00011B/59/P